ALL HALLOW'S EVE

❧

Mark Andrew Hunter

PublishAmerica
Baltimore

Hardcover 978-1-4512-6293-3
Softcover 978-1-4512-6294-0
PUBLISHED BY PUBLISHAMERICA, LLLP
www.publishamerica.com
Baltimore

Printed in the United States of America

Dedication

❧❧

To my lovely wife Lisa,
Thanks for putting up with me for all these years.

I

꒰ꙮ꒱

Wednesday October 23rd, 1991

Nicole Nicholson sat in her first period class at 8:18 a.m. listening to the University of Eastern Nebraska Biology I professor drone on about the internal structures of the cell. Actually, to say that she was sitting and listening was not quite true. Rather, Nicole was in her seat with her head resting upon the palm of her right hand (thus preventing her writing hand from doing anything as strenuous as note taking) allowing such phrases as cytoplasm, robosomes and the golgiaparatus to slip into her semi-conscious mind.

Nicole was a freshman at the college, majoring in liberal arts: which meant that she had no idea what to major in. However, at this moment she knew that she did *not* want to major in microbiology! In fact, what she really wanted to do right now was to compensate for the lack of sleep that she had missed out on by getting up at 6:00 a.m. She was just about to *over*-compensate for lack of sleep by taking a little siesta in her chair when suddenly, she was saved by the bell: 8:30 a.m., next period.

The next period was free, so Nicole sleepily sauntered over to the student lounge to lounge upon one of the plush sofas that she now found just too inviting to resist in her present sleep deprived condition. She was only going to lie down for a few minutes but…the next thing that she knew she had overslept and she was ten minutes late for her next class!

Wouldn't you know it: it was one of the few of her classes that she had this semester that actually could hold her attention: World Civilizations. So she sheepishly crept into the lecture hall and took a seat in the back row. After taking copious notes on the fall of the Roman Empire she was free to go to lunch. After she had feasted on the fine cuisine of the school cafeteria she went to get her mail.

Nicole found, to her surprise, that she had received a package. It was a large, common square cardboard box with packing tape affixed to it, with her name and the college's address written upon it. What was strange about the package was that there was no return address on it. It was not even near her birthday and Christmas was still a couple of months away. She supposed that it could be a care package from her parents, but why no return address? Who could have sent it? What was inside it?

Nicole stayed her curiosity long enough to carry the package back to her dorm room (at least it wasn't too heavy!). As soon as she was inside her room she opened it up. She sifted through the styrofoam packing peanuts and pulled out a stuffed toy. It was a grinning red devil complete with horns, goatee, pointy tail and holding a little plastic pitchfork. It was a funny gift to send to someone, particularly anonymously. Well, it *was* nearly Halloween and a gift was still a gift, even an anonymous one.

Nicole dug around in the styrofoam for a while longer but she still didn't find a card or note. She looked again all over the box: there was nothing on it but her name and the college's address written on it and she didn't recognize the handwriting. She decided it must have been sent from a secret admirer. But if so, wouldn't Cupid have been more apropos than Lucifer? Perhaps the besotted individual couldn't wait until St. Valentine's Day and this time of year this was all he or she could find.

Another odd thing about the item was that while it looked store bought, she could not find any toy manufacturer's name on it, no 'made in China', or any identifiable markings at all. Furthermore, Nicole had never even seen another stuffed toy devil quite like it before in any toy store, nor a souvenir shop or carnival or even on television ("not available in stores-order now!").

'Curiouser and curiouser' Nicole thought to herself, quoting Alice' apt (if rather grammatically incorrect) phrase from Lewis Carroll's immortal novel. If she were a more suspicious person she probably would had been freaked out by the entire situation; but she had an affinity for the macabre and the mysterious. At any rate, she found the toy quite charming and so she deposited it upon the headboard shelf above her bed.

For the next few days Nicole went about her usual business (getting up far too early, sleeping in class, attempting to ingest the swill served in the lunch room, etc.). She called her parents and asked her friends and acquaintances about the anonymous gift but no one admitted to sending the package. 'Where the hell did it come from'? She asked herself. Herself answered: 'Maybe that's *where* it came from.'

Nicole laughed at the thought. She had a healthy skepticism in regards to the supernatural. When pressed on the point she would admit to the possibility of the existence of a 'higher power'; but she didn't believe in any entity of ultimate evil by the name of Lucifer or Satan. She had an even harder time believing that the eternal abode of the damned doubled as a stuffed toy department!

Still, the little devil *was* a mystery. The most plausible answer was the secret admirer theory or else a college prank. The most disquieting aspect of all of this, in either case, was the question of what was to follow the present. And what if the sender's feelings were a little more menacing than simple tomfoolery or, maybe even more disquieting, more intense than mere 'admiration'?

Perhaps, the package was only the beginning, to be followed subsequently by 'love' letters, obscene phone calls, footsteps behind her in the dark of night, finally ending with her violent rape and murder and her body being found in some dark alley? But in the ensuing days and weeks, no other gifts were forthcoming from the mysterious sender, so it appeared to be an isolated incident.

II

ᔣ∽ᔥ

Nicole Nicholson was from Louisville, a small town in the southeast part of the Midwestern state of Nebraska. She had come to the college in Omaha partly to appease her parents but mostly to get out from under their protective wings. The parents in question were: Nicholas Alan Nicholson III, a college history professor and his wife Anne Marie (nee' Benson) an elementary school teacher.

Nicole was supposed to have been born Nicholas Alan Nicholson IV but genetics (and/or divine providence) conspired against Mr. Nicholson and the Nicholson's only child was born (on March the fifth, nineteen seventy-three): a girl. So they named her Nicole Alana Nicholson (the first?) instead. Though the Nicholsons tried hard to produce another child, infertility plagued the couple. As it was, Nicole was born when her parents were well into their forties.

The Nicholsons considered adoption but ultimately rejected the idea. Her father tried hard not to show his disappointment in not being able to produce a male heir and Nicole tried hard to make up for it by excelling in sports but her body was just not fit for the task. Still Nicole enjoyed her upper middle-class existence for the most part (at least until she started elementary school).

Nicole was a little on the short side (5'4") but appeared taller owing to her slender frame and her long, straight dark brown hair that she customarily wore parted on the right side. Her eyes were of a matching dark brown hue, which contrasted with her milky white complexion. Her paleness coupled with her slight frame and small features made her seem more fragile than she really was. Another of her contrasting features was her voice: where one might have expected a tiny little girl's voice to come from her tiny little girl's body what they heard instead was a husky contralto.

In terms of personality she was a little on the shy side. Nicole was wary of large groups of people; particularly due to the teasing and bullying that she had received while growing up. Few creatures are as systematically cruel as children are. Their favorite targets tend to be the different: the over-weight, the short, the handicap and the anorexically skinny. And if Nicole was unusually thin now, she was virtually a stick figure in grade school.

Not that Nicole was actually anorexic. In fact, she wanted nothing more than to get up to a reasonable 100 pounds. She was just one of those people who simply could not gain weight no matter how much she ate. To multiply her miseries she had her class-mates to add insult to injury. 'Nicky the Stick' they labeled her in first grade and the 'nick' name stuck. She gained other nicknames such as: 'Nicole the Beanpole' and several other worst ones too cruel to mention.

Of course she heard all of the jokes (example: Q: Why does 'Nicky the Stick' wear flippers in the shower? A: So that she doesn't slide down the drain). Then there was the graffiti, the insults, sometimes even physical abuse like the time some bullies tried to force-feed her their lunch in back of the school bus. In time, Nicole was also routinely kicked, knocked over and even spit upon.

So Nicole grew up withdrawn and sullen, trying as hard as she could be inconspicuous so that her classmates would just ignore her. What little friends that she possessed were the other misfits at school, the other targets of abuse. By high school Nicole had given up even trying to fit in, deciding that if she was going to be treated differently she would truly *be* different: in other words, if you can't join 'em, then beat 'em. Her way of beating them was to revel in her strangeness.

In high school she started listening to the 1950's jazz (particularly Be-Bop and Cool) that her father listened to and she began dressing all in black like a beatnik. She also liked to listen to her parent's younger sibling's late sixties 'hippie music' as well. It was musically as far away from Rap or 1980's heavy metal 'hair band' music as you could get.

Another way to beat them was to ignore their taunting and concentrate on her studies: natural sciences and mathematics aside; she was actually a good student. She did well in literature and the social sciences (history, sociology, psychology). Nicole particularly excelled in the arts: both the performing arts (music, drama) and the arts proper (painting, sculpture, photography). Obviously, she didn't excel at sports and she never even considered trying out for cheerleading!

Eventually Nicole learned to ignore her classmate's jibes and even to play along with them. She had found something within herself to counteract the damage inflicted upon her self-esteem: the worth of her own soul. Most of Nicole's classmates eventually grew up, as most people do, and developed more admirable traits such as responsibility and empathy. After a while some of them even took the trouble to get to know her and they discovered that she was an interesting, albeit an unusual, person.

So, Nicky the Stick became Nicole Nicholson the person. After she had gotten over some of her anti-social tendencies, Nicole could be a friendly person, smiling and saying 'hi' to whomever she met. If they didn't return her salutation she just figured it was *their* problem. So, Nicole had gotten to know many of her former tormentors and even tried to forgive them. As for her fellow students who never grew up and continued to harass her, she just learned to tolerate them.

***

However, Nicole was doing a little better in the friend department at the college. Living in a college dormitory was naturally conducive to generate feelings of amity (as well as enmity) with others. Living on the same hall with other people was like having another family: one could really get to know one another well. That didn't mean that everyone became great friends or even grew to like one another, but you either learned to live with it or else you moved out. Initially, you couldn't choose your hall mates (or even your roommates) but you could choose your friends.

And Nicole chose, or was chosen, enough at college to keep her from being lonely. Most of what passes for friendships are people who share common beliefs and interests and there were enough of those people to be found in college where conformity wasn't valued as much as it was in high school. Nicole found that her eccentricities were tolerated more at the university, if not actually encouraged; particularly among the art and theatre crowd. However, one may have many 'friends' in the superficial social sense of the word but close personal friendships are rare.

Nicole had only found one such friend so far during her freshman year: her next-door neighbor Amy Daniels. Like most best friends the two girls were total opposites, both in terms of personality and physicality. Amy was a big (5'-10"), beautiful, buxom, blue eyed, blond babe from the big city of Omaha. Amy was sociable, extroverted, and optimistic; traits that contrasted and complemented Nicole's solemn reserve. Amy's effervescent personality and good natured humor also offset Nicole's cynical sarcasm.

About the only thing that they had in common was their interest in philosophy, specifically metaphysics; and even then, they approached the subject from opposite ends of the spectrum. Despite her vivacious personality Amy was a deep thinker and a good student. At first, Nicole was surprised to find that her newfound friend was (of all things!) a born again Christian.

Amy Elizabeth Daniels was the daughter of David (a Conservative Baptist minister, for God's sake!) and his homemaker wife Amy. Amy Daniels II was the youngest of several children from a large working class family. She had even 'accepted Christ' at the age of five. Even though Amy had been raised in a Christian home she was not a spoon-fed blind faith believer. She had obviously thought through her convictions and believed that Biblical Christianity was the most rational worldview.

Amy was not a frothing-at-the-mouth religious nut; she was not a hypocritical holier-than-thou starched white shirt churchgoer. Nor was she an ascetic nun hiding away from the world in a cloister somewhere or a sanctimonious killjoy who didn't have any fun. She was a kind, compassionate person who lived out what she believed, enjoyed life and was not afraid of dissenters.

If Amy Daniels had been any of the negatives listed above she would not have been a best friend of Nicole Nicholson. Nicole could not stand intolerance, hypocrisy or absence of moderation in any organized fashion—no matter whether it was in the name of religion or atheism, conservatism or liberalism, white supremacists or black militants, male chauvinism or feminism, Republican or Democratic.

It was all the same to her. Nicole Nicholson was a firm believer in a free, pluralistic society—one which fell somewhere between totalitarianism and anarchy. She believed that a democracy only worked if all were tolerant of everyone else's beliefs (for a cynic she could be, at times, quite an idealist!).

Nicole herself had been raised by liberal atheists. Both of her parents had come from Omaha families that were well off and they had met at college and then spent their college days and following rebelling against their affluent backgrounds. In other words: they were something of Midwestern beatniks or hippies, though they had assimilated considerably since then. Nicole was a firm believer in her parent's precepts until she got to know people of other ideological persuasions and came to the conclusion that most systems of belief have a certain amount of truth to them.

So, Nicole developed an open mind and a certain talent for seeing other people's points of view and mediating between opposing sides. In other words, she had gone from being a liberal to a moderate, or perhaps more accurately, a pluralist. She did not whole-heartedly subscribe to any particular school of thought, preferring to keep an open mind on most subjects. She certainly wasn't ready to commit herself to any religious structure that was as rigid as Christianity (she was, in fact, currently leaning towards Buddhism) but she respected Amy's practice of what she preached.

***

Nicole and Amy had met at the beginning of the school year on the hall but they didn't get much past polite salutations at their first meeting whilst moving their personal belongings into their respective dorm rooms. They met again briefly that night at a social gathering at the beginning of the school year that freshmen were strongly encouraged to attend. They were also strongly encouraged to play various silly games designed to break down people's inhibitions.

Nicole had spent years constructing her defenses and she wanted to let them down only when *she* was ready; when she felt that it was safe. Nicole was instantly sorry that she had ever come to the event and she soon departed for the safety of her dorm room. Later that evening Nicole was in her bedroom, sitting 'Indian style' on her bed, reading J. D. Salinger's "Catcher in the Rye" (paperback edition) and listening to Jefferson Airplane's "After Bathing at Baxter's" (CD version).

The Airplane was just one of many great musical artists that Nicole had been turned onto by her aunts and uncles. It was 9:17 p.m.; Holden Caulfield had just finished his conversation with Mr. Spencer (end of chapter two) and the Airplane had just started "Won't You Try/ Saturday Afternoon" and Nicole's right foot was starting to get numb when her fun was interrupted by a gentle rapping upon her dorm room door.

After her experience earlier that evening Nicole was feeling less sociable than usual and she didn't like being interrupted in the middle of listening to a recording (at least she was at an end of a chapter in her book!), but she would never be so rude as to pretend that she was not home when she in fact was (she couldn't do so even if she wanted to since she was playing her stereo at top volume—though she could have used the excuse that she hadn't heard the knock over the musical din!).

So, Nicole reluctantly put her book down, turned down the volume on her CD player, got off of her bed and limped towards the door, remembering just why she usually avoided sitting cross-legged (!). She opened the door to Amy Daniel's smiling face.

"Hi. I saw you leaving the gathering early."

"I really don't really get into all that 'let's get acquainted' kind of crap, if you want to know the truth. I really don't. That stuff really bores me." (Nicole stated in Caulfield-ease; Nicole had the habit of getting into the book that she was reading so completely that she sometimes would even start talking like the protagonist of the novel—she was just lucky that she hadn't been reading Shakespeare!).

"I guess that it's not for everyone." Amy offered politely.

"No, it isn't. Won't you come in…um…I'm sorry, I've forgotten your name."

"Amy Daniels. And yours was Nicole Nicholson? Do you prefer Nicole or Nicky?"

"*Nicole,* definitely Nicole. Please don't ever call me Nicky!"

"Okay…sorry if I struck a nerve."

"It's alright, you didn't know. It's a long story. Why don't you come in and I'll tell you all about it."

So Amy came inside Nicole's dorm room. Nicole's room was done in late sixties hippie crash pad décor. She had the obligatory posters of such luminaries as Hendrix, Dylan and the Beatles. She had throw pillows on the bed, a beanbag on the floor and if she could have gotten away with it she probably would have painted her walls in bright psychedelic colors (and she maybe even would have had a hookah!).

Unlike most teenagers Nicole thought that the older generation were eternally cool and thus she never rebelled against her upbringing, preferring instead to rebel against her classmates musical tastes by getting into 1950's Jazz and 1960's hippie music. Her CD player had by this time switched to Jefferson Airplane's "Crown of Creation" CD and the song "Lather" (which she never really cared much for) was now playing.

"Hope you like the Airplane." Nicole warned.

"The what?" Amy innocently asked, looking around the room for a flying machine. (She herself has been raised on mostly hymns, contemporary Christian music and classical music).

"Never mind. Have a seat…on the bed or the beanbag, your choice."

Amy chose the bed as the safer of the two alternatives and Nicole took the beanbag; the two girls sat for hours talking about their respective upbringings and philosophies of life whilst Nicole worked her way thru the rest of her collection of Jefferson Airplane CDs (Just like her father, Nicole always liked to listen to a particular artist's entire catalogue in chronological order).

As far as their respective worldviews were concerned they both just agreed to disagree. They both liked to have friendly arguments, both believing that it helped each of them to clarify just what they believed and why they believed it. From that night onward they were the best of friends.

III

Thursday October 31st, 1991

October the 31st, the day before all saints day or alternately, all
hallow's eve, better known to most as Halloween. While growing up
Nicole's favorite holiday had always been Halloween. It wasn't just the
sweets or even the macabre nature of the holiday (though she loved both
of these aspects of the event).

The real reason that Nicole liked Halloween was that it gave her a
chance to pretend that she was someone else for the day. This aspect
was particularly important to her during her unhappy childhood. Nicky
the stick could become a beautiful fairy princess or she could wreak
vengeance on her tormentors as a wicked witch. She was also a closet
drama queen and really loved the dressing up part!

In the past week Nicole was finding that college life was, for the most
part, an enjoyable experience, though Biology I wasn't getting any
easier. However, she had just this very day found an unofficial biology
tutor in a fellow student and resident science whiz named Eric Spencer.
They were both in Biology I class together but Eric was having a much
better time of it than she was.

Though not an unattractive person by any means, being rather tall with black hair and blue eyes, Eric Spencer was an unusual boy, to say the least. He was brilliant, at least as far as academics were concerned. His social graces were another matter. Eric was painfully shy but that wasn't the entire problem. Eric was...odd.

Eric stood out in a crowd, or, to be more precise, apart from the crowd and maybe even above it. He didn't socialize much with people and he seemed to regard others as inferior to himself. He had a habit of observing other people in such a way that it reminded one of a scientist viewing a lower life form in a microscope. It was in fact this very habit of his which occasioned the coed's first proper introduction.

Nicole was sitting on one of the couches in the student lounge (lounging, but not sleeping this time) when she noticed a male student on the other side of the room looking intently at her. She found his attention a little disconcerting at first. So she decided to take the bull by the horns and defuse the situation by just going over there and talking to him. She found the voyeur in question vaguely familiar, and by the time that she got over to him and flopped down on the couch adjacent to the chair where he was sitting on, she was almost sure that she had placed him.

"Hi." She greeted cheerfully.

"H-hello." Eric stuttered, a little startled.

"I got it!" Nicole exclaimed in recognition as she snapped her fingers, "You're in my Biology I class!"

"That is correct." He answered, slightly more at ease.

"I thought so. You're one of those students who keep screwing up the grade curve! Your name is...don't tell me, let me guess...Rick?"

"Eric." He corrected, his voice betraying some annoyance that she had gotten his name wrong. "Eric Spencer."

"That's it! But, come on, I was a little close!"

"And you are Nicole Nicholson."

"Right the first time. I guess that you're just better with names than I am. So, Eric Spencer, I suppose that you aced that pop quiz we had yesterday?"

"Of course." Eric said in a manner that was at the same time both prideful and matter-of-fact. "How did you do?"

"Don't ask. I'm hopeless when it comes to science."

"Biology is not that hard. Of course, it would probably help you if you would stay awake during class."

"Very funny. Sure, it's easy for you to say that it's easy; you're obviously some sort of scientific genius. Personally, I'm petrified of the next test coming up. I already flunked the mid-term exam earlier this month."

"If you'd like I could go over the material with you sometime."

"I'd like that very much, Eric; but I don't have my Biology stuff with me today." (The Biology I class met on Mondays, Wednesdays and Fridays).

"That's okay. I got the textbook in my backpack. Though I'm not sure why I have it; besides the fact that I don't have Biology class today, I've got most of the information in my head most of the time anyway."

So Nicole and her newfound friend spent a couple of hours reviewing the material, as well as getting to know each other through the various bunny trails that Nicole found so much more interesting than the subject that they were *supposed* to be studying. The new friends found that they had much in common:

They were both only childs. They were both shy and socially awkward, though Eric seemed to be much more so than Nicole was. They both shared an interest in the horror and science fiction genre (Nicole liked science fiction, it was science *fact* that she despised!), both in terms of literature and cinema. They also both possessed a dry, wry sense of humor.

After a couple of hours of study Nicole announced:

"Okay, that's about all that my head can take of this subject for now!"

"Are you sure?" Eric asked apprehensively. The truth of the matter was that he didn't want their time together to end so soon.

"Yea. I appreciate your tutelage and all and I think that's its really going to help…but I want to get ready for the dance tonight. Are you going?"

"I wasn't planning on it."

"What's the matter? You're not one of those conservative Christian types who have religious convictions against Halloween and/or dancing, are you?"

"I am not religious. I'm just against dances as a matter of principle…owing to the fact that I can't dance." Eric added sheepishly.

"It's certainly easier than biology! Tell you what: since you helped me out with my Biology I lesson why don't I give you some pointers on dancing?"

"I…don't know…" Eric hesitated.

"Aw, come on, it will be fun!"

Nicole jumped off of the couch and managed to coax Eric up out of his chair. Then she showed him where to put his hands (on her hips) and she tried to put her arms around his neck, which wasn't easy since he was well over six feet tall! Nicole showed Eric how to do a basic 'box step' and Eric tried to not mangle Nicole's feet too badly by stepping on her toes. As for Nicole, she tried not to giggle too much during the process. Eric found that Nicole was right: dancing *was* fun. In fact, he didn't want the experience to end.

After their dancing lesson was over Nicole inquired:

"So, have I removed your objections for going to the dance tonight?"

"I'll be there with bells on." Eric answered.

"Why, are you coming as a jester? Speaking of which: are you even going to have the time to dig up a costume this late?"

"I know where I can get one on short notice."

"Great. See you tonight."

***

As Nicole had mentioned: in honor of Halloween the college was having a masquerade party/dance. She decided to go to the masque dressed as a ghoul. She dressed all in black and applied white make-up to her face and hands and applied black lipstick, eye shadow and finger nail polish. Once her transformation was complete, she went over to Amy's room. She had been somewhat surprised to learn that Amy didn't have a problem with Halloween or dancing like some Christians she'd heard of and she was glad that she didn't have to go stag to the dance.

Amy's room, in contrast to Nicole's, was an oasis of sweetness: all cute stuffed toys and posters of pretty animals with even prettier platitudes printed upon them (usually uplifting Bible verses). All very pink and fluffy. In place of Nicole's bookshelf filled with Kerouac, Ginsberg, McClure, Ferlinghetti and other beat writers, Amy's bookshelf was filled with bibles and authors that Nicole had never heard of like C.S. Lewis and Frank Peretti.

Amy was dressed up as an angel: full-length white robe complete with a sparkly silver halo and fluffy white wings. When Nicole had poked her ghoulish head into her friend's room, Amy asked:

"What do you think?"

"I think that you have an exalted opinion of yourself."

"Just wishful thinking. And what are you supposed to be: a zombie?"

"Close; I'm a ghoul."

"What's the difference?"

"A ghoul is a spirit that feeds upon dead bodies. A zombie is a re-animated corpse."

"Oh…well, you look more like a rock musician to me."

"Yea, I suppose that I do look like a refugee from the band Kiss."

"Let us now depart for the party then." Amy suggested.

The two young ladies arrived at the school gymnasium at the fashionably late time of 7:10 p.m. Also at the dance was Eric Spencer, standing apart, dressed as Count Dracula. Nicole decided to introduce her two friends, so she grabbed Amy by the arm and dragged her over to the corner where Eric was standing and observing the goings on.

"Nice suit, Eric. Who's your tailor?" Nicole quipped.

"I'll have you know this suit has been in my family for generations."

"Right; just make sure that you return it to the costume store before mid-night or you'll have to pay for another night. Let me introduce the two of you: Eric Spencer, my science tutor and newfound friend, meet my next door neighbor and best friend: Amy Daniels."

20

"Pleased to meet you." Amy said cheerfully as the two of them shook hands.

"Watch out, Eric, she's a born-again-Christian type." Nicole warned.

Eric quickly let go of Amy's hand and stepped backwards; the three of them all laughed. Then Eric appraised the two young women.

"You two are a rather incongruitous pair. An angel and a…ghoul?"

"Good guess." Nicole confirmed, "I'm just an all-American ghoul."

"You're the coolest ghoul in school." Amy interjected merrily.

"Your puns are going to be the death of this party." Eric groaned. Then he suggested:

"You two should have come dressed up as an angel and a she-devil to make the contrast even greater."

"I guess that we'll just have to synchronize our costumes better the next year." Nicole mused.

After conversing for a while the dancing commenced. Eric begged off for most of the night, again protesting that he couldn't dance, but Nicole was persistent and got him out on the dance floor a couple of times towards the end of the evening. However, Eric wasn't employing false modesty: he really couldn't dance.

Neither Amy nor Nicole had to sit out too many dances though, being as they were both, in their diverse ways, pretty enough girls. Amy particularly seemed to get repeat invitations to dance from certain male coeds. The masque was over by 10:00 p.m. and then Eric escorted the two young ladies back to the women's dormitory.

"Are you tired yet?" Amy asked when the two girls had gone up the stairs and reached their hallway on the third floor of Johnson hall.

"Not particularly." Nicole answered.

"Then let's go to my room and talk."

Amy took Nicole by the arm and dragged her inside her room. After closing the door Amy flopped down upon her bed and signed.

"I felt like the belle of the ball tonight."

"You certainly didn't lack for a partner for too long." Nicole confirmed as she sat down on the bed next to Amy.

"You didn't do too badly yourself."

"No, I guess that I didn't at that. I'm just not used to getting all of that male attention."

"So many men, so little time."

"Amy! And I thought that you were a good Christian girl."

"I *am* a good Christian girl. I was talking about dancing. Just *what* were you implying?"

"Sorry. But the dance was fun."

"I could have danced all night."

"You did. I myself was never asked to any dances in high school so I guess that this makes up for it."

"I find that hard to believe; you're a pretty girl."

"Thank you." Nicole blushed. "So are you."

"It was obvious that what's his name…Eric, is it…hasn't been to too many dances."

"Don't make fun of him. Eric tried. Besides, he's never danced before tonight. I just taught him some steps this very afternoon."

"Oh, is there something that I should know about you two?"

"We're just friends."

"Then is there someone else that you wanted to dance with instead?"

"I'm going to have to plead the fifth on that one." Nicole said, blushing even more. Then she switched the question around and asked Amy:

"What about you?"

"I haven't narrowed it down yet. I guess that I'll see which one of them asks me out first. May the best man win!"

"You're terrible! But I guess that I'd better toddle off to bed now. We do still have classes tomorrow, remember?"

"Unfortunately, yes we do." Amy conceded.

"Goodnight then until tomorrow: 'Parting is such sweet sorrow.'

"Goodnight, Romeo. Or are you Juliet?"

"Right now I'm just plain tired. Goodnight, sweet princess, or I should say, sweet angel?"

IV

⚜

Friday November 1ˢᵗ, 1991

Amy had been soundly asleep for a few hours when she was awakened by a high-pitched noise. In her barely awoken, disoriented state of mind she at first thought it was her alarm clock going off. A quick inspection of said clock, however, revealed that this was a false assumption; it also revealed that it was 3:47 a.m.

By this time Amy was awake enough to determine that the noise that she heard was in fact a blood-curdling scream! She jumped out of bed, threw on a robe and her fluffy bunny slippers and stumbled out into the hallway, noticing that the scream seemed to emanating from Nicole's room. Amy opened the door (thankfully, Nicole hadn't locked it), burst through the doorway and groped for the light switch. Finding the switch she turned on the lights, fearing just what she might see.

Amy did not, however, see an intruder engaged in the process of murdering her best friend in her own bed (as she had half expected to). Amy further looked around the room and she didn't find any intruder hiding in Nicole's closet or signs that her window had been broken into. What Amy did see was the sight of her best friend sitting straight up in bed, drenched in sweat and screaming at the top of her lungs.

Amy quickly surmised that, even though Nicole's eyes were wide open, she must be asleep and experiencing a horrific nightmare. By this time, most of Nicole's hall mates were also awake and were stumbling out into the hallway or poking their heads out their respective doorways, wondering just what the commotion was. Some were soon poking their heads into Nicole's doorway. After several seconds Amy succeeded in waking Nicole up by grabbing her by the shoulders and shaking her vigorously.

"Nicky…um…Nicole, Wake up! Are you all right?"

"Huh…what? Amy? What are you doing here? And why is everybody up and in my room? Is there a fire?"

"Everything is all right." Amy cooed.

By this time half of their hall mates were in Nicole's room, sleepily (and some angrily) staring at Nicole and murmuring amongst themselves. Amy could tell that this further alarmed Nicole so she calmed down the other girls and tactfully ushered them out of the room and closed the door behind them. When she turned back to the bed she could see that Nicole was now fully awake and looking quite confused. Amy sat down on the bed beside her and taking Nicole by the hand and laying her hand on Nicole's cheek she asked:

"Are you sure that you are okay?"

"I…I'm not sure. What happened?"

"You were having a nightmare is all. Do you remember what you dreamt about?"

Nicole's brow furrowed as she tried to remember.

"It's no use! It's a complete blank. Was I talking in my sleep?"

"Not…exactly…" Amy hesitated.

"What did I do? Tell me!"

"You were…screaming."

"Screaming? Freaky! God, my nightgown is drenched. I must have been sweating like a proverbial pig. And it's October!"

"Actually, it's November 1st, about 4:00 a.m., in fact."

"No wonder everyone was looking at me with daggers in their eyes. They all have to get up for their classes! And so do we, in about two hours."

"Are you sure that you're up to it?"

"I guess so, though it looks like I'm going to be sleeping in class again."

"Just as long as you don't start screaming in class."

"I'll save that for when I get my grades at the end of the semester."

"Glad to see that you're keeping your sense of humor."

"I'd rather have some more sleep instead. In fact, I think that I'll try to catch some more Zs now before its 6 a.m."

"Would you like me to stay with you?"

"You've already done enough, Am. Thank you for your kindness."

"Forget it. I'm your friend. I care about you."

"You're truly an angel."

"And you're a good little ghoul. Now try to get some sleep."

"See you tomorrow…or rather in a few hours."

"Pleasant dreams." Amy wished.

"I hope." Nicole replied.

***

Nicole didn't get back to sleep, however. She was too worried about what had just happened. What could she have dreamt of that could have caused her to scream bloody murder? She wasn't *that* worried about her classes, not even the ones that she should've been worried about! Certainly the party hadn't scared her that much. And she didn't believe that Halloween had anything to do with it; she didn't believe that evil spirits were getting their kicks by possessing or oppressing her on their favorite holiday.

Eventually, Nicole just gave up on getting anymore sleep and so she got up. She then took a shower, got dressed in a pair of blue jeans, a black turtle neck sweater and white tennis shoes, she ran a comb through her arrow straight hair, threw on a light jacket to ward off the mid-autumn morning chill and went off to her first class: the dreaded Biology I. Her lack of sleep soon caught up with her and she was soon sleeping like a baby, but at least there was no screaming involved. Her experiences in her other classes didn't go much better.

After classes Nicole again had a biology lesson with Eric in the student lounge, after which he asked her to accompany him to return his costume. She readily agreed and they got into his 1988 silver Chevy Citation and drove down to the heart of Omaha's downtown district: the historic Old Market area. Once they had parked the car, (no mean feat even on a weekday afternoon) and fed the parking meter they walked over the brick streets and came to an ancient brick edifice. The plate glass window on the storefront was embossed with the legend: Spencer's Olde Novelty Shoppe.

Inside was a quaint little shop(pe) with novelties, knickknacks, cards and costumes; as you would expect, mostly related to the holiday of Halloween. For a minute Nicole wondered if the business was associated with the national chain of the same name but she quickly dismissed the idea. This was plainly a family owned business. It took only a few minutes more for Nicole to make the connection between the store's name and Eric.

"So you see, Nicole, I wasn't exaggerating very much when I said that this costume has been in my family for generations."

Eric handed over the costume, across the counter, to the store's proprietor. The proprietor in question looked like an older version of Eric with the same tall, lanky frame, black hair (except for a distinguished graying of the temples) and cold steel blue eyes. As he took the costume, he inquired with a detectable English accent:

"I trust that my count Dracula costume was a success."

"Yes, father, it made quite an impression." Eric answered.

"You'll have to forgive my son's manners, Miss. Eric, I believe that introductions are in order."

"Nicole, this is my father, Mr. Edmund Spencer. Father, may I present to you Miss Nicole Nicholson, a friend from college."

"Ah, yes, Miss Nicholson, at last we meet." Mr. Spencer said with a smile as he proffered his hand. "My son has spoken so often about you." (At this revelation Eric seemed rather uncomfortable).

"Really? I must have made quite an impression since we've only recently become acquainted." Nicole said as she took Mr. Spencer's hand. The elder Mr. Spencer then bowed and kissed her hand. Nicole blushed, then smiled and said:

"Pleased to meet you Mr. Spencer. I can see where Eric gets his good looks from." (Eric colored at this last remark).

"Flattery will get you everywhere. And please call me Edmund; 'Mr. Spencer' was my father."

"And you can call me Nicole. Just don't call me Nicky!"

Nicole observed that while father and son looked nearly identical, the father possessed a certain flamboyance and social grace that his son lacked.

"This is quite an interesting store you have here Mr. Spenc…er…Edmund. I would assume that you do great business this time of year."

"You assume correctly, Miss Nicole. This is my favorite time of the year and not only due to financial considerations."

"Mine too. Next Halloween I'll have to come here. I'm so glad to see that you haven't taken down the Halloween decorations yet."

"I am always loath to do so. I think that they are so much more aesthetically pleasing than turkeys, pilgrims and American Indians."

"Anyway, your son looked positively diabolical last night."

"And the costume was scary too." Eric quipped.

"Still have that self-deprecating sense of humor, eh son?'

"We'd better be going, Dad." Eric said abruptly.

"Farewell, Eric, and nice to meet you Nicole. Stop by anytime."

"Love to. I like the ambiance of the place." Nicole answered.

On the way back to the college, Nicole observed:

"Eric, your father is simply charming! How come you've never mentioned him before?"

"You've never asked."

"Okay: I'm asking now."

"Let's just say that we've had something of a falling out after my mother died."

"I'm sorry. I…I didn't know."

"How could you know; I've never told you." Eric said petulantly.

The two of them drove awhile in silence. Then Eric broke the silence.

"Sorry, Nicole; I guess I sounded a little bitter there."

"I…didn't mean to pry."

"It's all right. I guess that I'm not much into self disclosure."

"You don't have to tell me about it if you don't want to."

"Maybe I will…someday."

The two new friends rode the rest of the way back to campus mostly in silence, where Eric deposited Nicole back at her dormitory building. After doing some studying and having dinner in the cafeteria, Nicole made an early night of it in order to catch up on some of her lost sleep.

V

Saturday November 2ⁿᵈ, 1991

It was late that night or rather early the next morning (2:52 a.m. to be exact) when Amy awoke, positively parched. Thankfully, it was due to a dry throat (rather than any high pitch screaming) that her sleep was disturbed. So Amy got up and walked to the drinking fountain down the hall, on the way back to her room she decided to check up on Nicole. She deftly opened the door and peered into the room. Once again she found Nicole sitting up in bed.

"What do you want?" Nicole asked.

Amy was startled by the sudden voice. Thinking Nicole was talking to her she was about to apologize for disturbing her friend when she realized that Nicole was once again asleep. *She's just talking in her sleep again,* Amy thought, *well, at least it's better than screaming.*

"What do you want from me?"

Amy was becoming concerned. Nicole's voice sounded frightened.

"Please just leave me alone!"

Nicole's voice was becoming shriller, she was now terrified! Amy, afraid that it was about to become a repeat of last night, began shaking Nicole, though not as roughly as the night before.

"Let go of me!!" Nicole screamed.

Nicole began to struggle against Amy's grip. Her face had contorted to a mask of mortal terror. Amy shook Nicole harder until her struggling had ceased.

"W-what? A-Amy? Oh my God! I've had another nightmare?"

"Now calm down Nicole. It's all right."

"All right?! I've just had two nightmares in as many nights and you say that it's all right?"

"Shh. Now you don't want to wake up the entire hall again."

"I haven't been screaming again, have I?"

"Not yet. Just talking in your sleep."

"What did I say? Tell me!"

"Something like: 'Get away from me'. You were pretty frightened. You seemed to be fighting or trying to get away from something…or someone."

"But from what or…whom?"

"You tell me."

"I…I don't know…"

"You mean that you don't remember…again?"

"It's…all so hazy…all that I remember is that it was horrible, like I was in hell or something." With that Nicole broke down and wept.

"Oh Amy, what am I going to do?"

Amy put her arm around her and advised:

"Don't start cracking up here, everybody has nightmares."

"Not like these!"

"Did you ever talk in your sleep or anything like that when you were growing up?"

"Not that I've ever been told."

"It's probably just nerves. Adjusting to college life or something."

"You really think so?"

"Of course I do. You'll see, just give it a few more nights and you'll be sleeping like a baby." Amy only wished that she was as confident as she sounded. She was actually beginning to worry about Nicole herself.

"Maybe you're right, Am. Anyway, thank you again. You're too good to me…or too good for me."

"Nobody can be *too* good."

Nicole looked at her clock radio.

"It's after 3:00 o'clock in the morning. We'd better both get back to bed."

"Are you sure that you'll be okay now?"

"How could I not be okay with my guardian angel watching over me?"

"I'm no angel; but I am your friend."

"A true friend. Good night sweet princess."

"Good night and may flights of angels sing *thee* to thy rest."

***

Nicole woke up later that morning after sleeping until later than noon, feeling quite refreshed. One of the joys of Saturday mornings was the ability to *really* sleep in. Later that afternoon Nicole took the bus downtown. She took the bus because she didn't own a car and even if she had she probably would have took the bus anyway because she knew she wouldn't have had a proverbial snowball's chance in Hades of getting a decent parking space downtown on a Saturday afternoon.

After walking around for a while on the brick laden streets of the old market area and even going into a few stores (including a couple of book stores housed in antique looking buildings which housed even more antique looking books) she found herself in front of Spencer's store, which was strange since she had no intention of going there!

Once Nicole saw Mr. Spencer's Shoppe, however, she decided to go on in. Once inside the store, she found a young couple talking to Mr. Spencer, speaking in low voices. Nicole was not prone to eves dropping so she didn't hear any of the conversation except the very end of it:

"See you tonight at the meeting, Edmund." One of the couple said as they were departing. After they had departed Mr. Spencer turned to Nicole and jovially exclaimed:

"Miss Nicholson! What brings you back so soon to my humble store?"

"Oh, I was just in the neighborhood."

"And I thought that you were developing a crush on me."

"You found me out: just *why* do think that I was in the neighborhood in the first place?"

"Watch out with that flirting, young lady or I just might just start to believe you."

"Actually, since I'm already here, I have a question to ask you."

"Ask away."

"Well, you seem to stock some rather…eccentric products here, so I was wondering if you have something like a stuffed devil."

"Yes, I'm sure we must have something like that here. Just walk this way fair young maiden."

"If I could walk that way I wouldn't be a fair young maiden."

Mr. Spencer led Nicole back to a clearance aisle with various Halloween items: cards, costumes, etc and stuffed toys. The obsolescence of the items was indicated by their low sale prices. Nicole saw several ghosts, jack o' lanterns, Frankenstein's monsters, vampires and yes, a myriad of red devils. But none of them looked exactly like hers.

'I've been trying to unload these lovelies since Halloween. I over-stocked as usual and now I can't *give* them away. Did you find what you were looking for?"

"Nope. None of these are what I'm looking for. Do you have any other product?"

"Not that I recollect. But it's possible that I could have sold out one or two models completely. But if you're looking for a gift for someone: any of these should do nicely."

"Oh, no, actually it's the other way around. I had received a stuffed devil and I'm trying to get any info I can to trace it back to the sender."

"An anonymous gift? How very mysterious."

"Quite. You don't happen to keep records of your sales by any chance? Or, at least, I imagine that you should have inventory of your stock."

"Certainly."

Mr. Spencer walked to the back of the store where there was

wooden door; he then produced an ancient looking skeleton key and opened the door that led to a small room. Inside the room was a big oak desk with a roll away cover, an antique swivel chair and a tall metal filing cabinet. Obviously the room served as his office. At the back of the room was another door. Mr. Spencer sat down on the swivel chair and started going through a book. Nicole was not surprised that he had no computer; it would have been incongruitous with the rest of his antique décor.

"We would have copies of receipts with the bar code information on it. Obviously I couldn't very well go back too far, I wouldn't have kept the receipt and I wouldn't have the time, if I did. When did you receive the item?"

"October the 23rd."

"Assuming that the buyer purchased the item recently and from this shop, I may be able to assist you. Of course, I would need the bar code. You would either need to bring in the item so I could get the bar code off of it or you could write it down and call it in to me."

"That's just it: there wasn't any bar code."

"No bar code? Perhaps it's a rather old item. How about a serial number then?"

"None."

"Manufacturer's name? A watermark? Anything?"

"Nothing that I can find."

"Then I would suggest that the item is homemade."

"Maybe you're right. But it sure doesn't look like it."

"Perhaps, it is a very well made homemade item."

"Thanks for trying anyway."

"You're welcome. But if you really want to thank me: buy something."

Nicole bought a decorative ceramic jack o' lantern candleholder that wasn't too expensive and Mr. Spencer rang it up on his antique cash register and then Nicole took her purchase with her and caught the next bus back uptown to the university. Nicole didn't mind traveling by bus since it gave her a chance to catch up on her reading. She was almost finished with "Catcher In The Rye" (chapter 25 Holden and Phoebe at the museum of art) and was anxious to finish it.

Nicole always experienced conflicting emotions when reading a book: desiring to finish the book versus wanting to savor the experience. Whenever she finished a book she felt both elation that she had finished it and regret that it was all over; after all, you can never again have the joy of reading a book for the first time; as the saying goes: you can't have your cake and eat it too.

Back at the college she once again met Eric in the student lounge for another biology cramming session.

"Hi, Eric." She said cheerfully as she sat down, "Guess where I've just been to."

"How the devil am I supposed to know?"

"Spoil sport. Actually, that was a good guess: I've just been to your father's store."

"Why did you go back there so soon?"

"You sound as if you don't approve."

"I just don't want you to be deceived."

"Deceived by a charming middle-aged man?"

"Yes! Fooled by his charm into thinking that he *is* just a harmless middle aged man."

"If you're so against him why did you bring me to see him? You even rented a costume from him!"

"Actually, I borrowed it. The reason I did so is that I am still trying to keep the lines of communication open with him. Besides, I needed a costume post haste for the dance. Why I brought you along with me to return it, I don't know. I wish now that I hadn't done either."

"But why? And how did you and your father become so estranged in the first place?"

Eric took a deep breath and then launched into his tragic tale:

"My father was a British business man who came to this country without the proverbial two pence to rub together in his pocket. He became a modest success in a few short years and met and married my mother. In the fullness of time he sired me, his only child. We had a happy home once, my parents loved each other and me and

I loved them. That all ended when I was thirteen years old when my mother contracted a malignant form of cancer.

"It was a long and painful illness that took its' toll on all of us. My father spent most of his resources on a fruitless attempt to cure her, but to no avail. My father and I could only watch helplessly as the disease slowly killed her. We took our frustrations out on each other. I began to stay away from home more and more because I couldn't deal with what was happening. Father interpreted this as lack of love and concern for my mother.

"At length, my mother succumbed to the disease. It was almost a blessing considering what she had been through. After mother's death father began to change: he lost his faith. Before that he was an Episcopalian, not very devout, perhaps, but he at least had a basic belief in God. As did I; he wasn't the only who lost his faith. I could not fathom how a good God could allow my pious mother to suffer the way that she had!

"Father and I had both prayed for God's deliverance but it never came. As a result I became an atheist. Father, however, began to search other religious systems for the answer to the afterlife; it became an obsession with him. Finally, he found a religious system that he believed gave him power, that allowed him to be God, a religion that allowed him to decide what was moral or immoral. And to him now *nothing* is immoral!

"Now my father and I are more estranged than ever before. After his conversion he took what was left of his money and opened up his little shop. But the shop is really only a front for his real passion in life. He wants me to join him in the 'family business' but I won't be a party to his abominable religious practices! And that is why I warn you: stay away from my father and his damnable shop!"

With that Eric stood up and strode out of the student lounge. Nicole sat there dumbfounded. She already knew that Eric was a little different but this was something else altogether. Either he was being melodramatic or her life had been a veritable picnic as compared to his! It certainly explained a lot about his anti-social personality. At any rate, she figured that the biology lesson for today was a bust.

So she trudged back over on the leaf covered streets to her dormitory and up to her dorm room. Nicole decided against confiding in Amy about the issue; she didn't feel that she was at liberty to discuss Eric's history with her. Besides, she also had the distinct impression that Eric only tolerated Amy for her own sake and that Amy's faith put him off (though she was never pushy about it).

After her conversation with Eric, Nicole needed to do something to take her mind off of it, not to mention her nocturnal troubles of late. So, Amy and she took in dinner and a movie: G rated for Amy's sake and *not* a horror movie for both of their sakes (Nicole was getting her daily requirement of horror from her nightmares!); then they headed back to their dorm and went to their respective bed rooms to sleep.

VI

Saturday November 2ⁿᵈ, 1991, evening

Nicole had had tension headaches, sinus headaches; even migraines but she had *never* in her life had had a headache such as this! She had been sleeping peacefully until just before eleven o' clock p.m. when she was awakened by a dull ache between her eyes. At first she just took a couple of aspirin and lay back down. Only the pain didn't go away, it just got worse, *much* worse. It soon grew to a violent throbbing ache that covered the entire surface of her face.

Eventually, Nicole was in so much pain that she was in tears; it was all that she could do to keep from screaming out loud (she didn't want to wake her neighbors again!). Suddenly, her door began to slowly creak open, Nicole stared at the door with some degree of trepidation until she saw Amy at the other side of the door. Amy whispered:

"Hey, Nick, how are you doing?"

Amy didn't even have to wait for a verbal reply to her inquiry. The answer was plainly etched upon Nicole's troubled face.

"What's the matter?" Amy asked.

"The…pain…" Nicole painted. Even speaking hurt.

"Where?"

"My…head…oh god…it hurts!"

"Have you tried taking something for it?"

"Extra strength…hours ago…didn't help…"

Amy couldn't stand to see anyone in such pain, particularly not a good friend. Normally, she would have seen this as just a physical ailment but with all that Nicole had been going through lately Amy thought, perhaps, that it was something else: emotional, psychological, or even spiritual.

"Nicole, I have an idea. It's a little radical."

"Anything…to take way…pain."

"It's called 'lying on of hands.'"

"Who are you…Oral Roberts?"

"I don't believe in faith healers either; I do, however, believe that God heals those who have faith in Him."

"Enough theology…more practice."

Amy cradled Nicole's aching head upon her lap and gently laid her hands on her forehead as she prayed:

"Heavenly Father, please hear the prayer of your humble servant and deliver this poor child from her torment. I ask this in the name of your Blessed Son the Lord Jesus Christ. Amen."

Amy sounded very fervent, if a trifle melodramatic. For a while nothing seemed to change. Nicole thought that the whole thing was bunk. Maybe it required faith on *her* part as well. In which case, it definitely was *not* going to work: Nicole couldn't believe in something just for the sake of convenience. Suddenly, though, she began to feel a tingling sensation on her forehead and felt something almost like a presence. Slowly, she began to feel a slight abatement of the pain. A few minutes later, the ache had subsided completely.

"It worked! Oh, thank you Amy!"

"Don't thank me, thank God." Amy suggested.

"Thank you whoever or whatever you are, wherever you are."

"I guess that that's an improvement over atheism."

"Actually, I was never really an atheist; I'm an agnostic." Nicole explained.

"Whatever. At least now you may be more open to the suggestion of the existence of God."

"There are more things in heaven and earth than are dreamt of in my philosophy?"

"Something cured your headache, Horatio."

"The power of suggestion, perhaps?"

"Perhaps." Amy conceded.

"Do you think that I may be going crazy? Having hysterical headaches and night terrors?"

"The way that I see it, we have three alternatives: One, the headache was a physical problem and the pain reliever just happened to finally kick in. Two, it was all psychosomatic and my prayer just worked on some psychological level. Or, three, it was a spiritual manifestation and you really were healed by God."

"Assuming that it *is* spiritual: what does it all mean?"

"First of all, when did all of this start?"

"Around Halloween."

"Didn't you get that package around then?"

"The little Devil? C'mon, you're not going to tell me that the stuffed toy has anything to do with it!"

"You yourself said that it was mysterious."

"But why me? Why am *I* being tormented?"

"I don't know. But I suspect that everything that has been happening to you is somehow connected and it is connected to that stuffed toy devil."

"Okay. I'm going to give it a few more days and if it doesn't stop then I'm either going to see a doctor, a shrink or an exorcist!"

"And I'll pray for you that you will not endure any more afflictions."

"With you and God on my side: how can I possibly loose?"

"That's the spirit. Now, are you sure that you're all right, no more headache?"

"I'm fine. In fact, I feel better now than I have felt in days. Thanks again for all that you have done for me."

"What are friends for?" Amy asked rhetorically.

The two girls stayed up for awhile and talked until around midnight, when Amy decided to go off to bed (after all, she had to get up early the next morning in order to get up for church). Nicole stayed up a little bit longer in order to read her Biology I text book (she wasn't all that tired since she had slept to past noon that day and she *wasn't* planning on going to church the next morning!). Being as she found the subject of biology about as stimulating as watching the corn grow, she was soon drowsy enough so she went back to bed and fell back to sleep.

VII

⚜

Sunday November 3rd, 1991

The next morning Nicole got up late feeling quite rested. Amy had already gotten up much earlier and had gotten all dressed up in her Sunday best and was off to church. She had invited Nicole to go to church with her the night before but Nicole had begged off; she wasn't so convinced of the existence of a higher power as to make that kind of sacrifice as of yet!

After having had a leisurely shower and performing her usual morning grooming routine, Nicole went down to the school cafeteria for the weekly Sunday brunch. As she was waiting in line, Eric arrived. Nicole was a little apprehensive since she didn't know where she stood with him after their last conversation. She forsook her place in line and risked going over to him.

"Um…look, Eric, I'm sorry if I was a little too pushy yesterday…I…didn't mean to pry…"

"Forget about it, I've already have. I guess that it's just a sore subject."

"Still friends?"

"Of course. Listen…have you eaten brunch yet?"

"About ready to."

"Let's forget about this slop then. Do you like Chinese food?"

"I love it."

"Then let me take you away from all of this."

The two of them went to a Chinese restaurant that was located downtown called the Peking Palace. It was one of those grand old Chinese restaurants decorated in authentic Chinese décor with pretty Chinese waitresses dressed in authentic Chinese garb. After a delicious Chinese meal (almond chicken for Nicole, pepper steak for Eric and they split an order of crab Rangoon as an appetizer), they were then brought two complementary fortune cookies.

After they had cracked open their respective cookies Nicole inquired:

"What does your fortune say?"

"It says, quote: 'Wise is the man who is content in what life bestows upon him'. I don't much like the sound of that. It sounds like a warning of bad news."

"It sounds more like a proverb or a platitude than a fortune to me. At any rate, maybe you should just accept it and be content like it advises."

"It's just a scrap of paper." Eric pointed out.

"*My* scrap of paper says: 'The answer that you seek will soon be revealed'."

"Now *that* sounds like a fortune." Eric observed.

"A rather specific fortune at that." Nicole added.

"Especially for a scrap of paper stuffed inside an oddly shaped cookie."

"It is odd though, usually fortunes are more generic. This one sounds like one of those daily horoscopes that you find in the newspaper." Nicole mused aloud.

"Strange." Eric agreed.

"A lot of strange things have been happening to me lately." Nicole said under her breath.

"Like what?" Eric, who had overheard her, inquired.

"Never mind. Do you want to leave now?"

"Sure. Lunch was on me, though."

"Okay, but I'll get the tip." Nicole argued.

As they drove back up to the university Eric and Nicole did some small talking but, as they neared the college campus, Eric's voice took on a more serious tone.

"Nicole, you know that I consider you a true friend…"

"Thank you, Eric. I feel the same way about you."

"But…my feelings for you go a lot deeper than that…I think that I'm in love with you."

"But, Eric, you hardly know me."

"I know you well enough. I know that you are a beautiful, caring person. And…I think that you and I are right for each other. We have so much in common in our preferences, our personalities, our backgrounds…"

"Eric…this is all so sudden…I don't know what to say…"

"Say that you feel the same way."

"I…can't say that because I *don't* feel the same way. I'm sorry, Eric, I like you as a friend but that's all."

"Don't you think that you could ever love me someday?"

"Not in the way that you want me to. It's not you, Eric, it's me. You see…I've never really been into guys all that much…"

"You're all the same! You lead someone on and then when you're done using them you just drop them!"

"How can you say that?" Nicole gasped.

"Because it's true! I believed in you and you never really cared!"

"That's not true! I *do* care about you, Eric…only as a friend."

"Yeah? I've heard that one before; save it for the next sucker."

"Eric, please don't do this! I don't want to lose your friendship."

"Knock off the crocodile tears. Maybe you can shed some *real* tears when I make *you* hurt as much as you've hurt me!"

"Eric, don't let it end this way…"

"Just get out of my car; you can walk the rest of the way!"

Nicole reluctantly did as she was told, feeling hurt and confused. Luckily, they were not far from the college. Eric angrily sped off as

Nicole walked back to campus, dumbfounded. She had no idea that Eric felt that way, though there were signs if she had bothered to pay attention to them. Admittedly, she might have even missed signs of neon brightness since she had never inspired feelings of amore in anyone before; at least not as far as she knew.

Had she lead Eric on? Certainly, she had not done so consciously. She had been too busy trying to keep her own amorous feelings for Amy Daniels in check to even consider what Eric's feeling might be for her. When she got back to the dorm she made a beeline for Amy's room. Amy could tell right away that her friend was distraught.

"Nicole, what's the matter?"

"Eric and I just had a big fight."

"I'm sorry to hear that. What was the fight about?"

"It seems that Eric has certain feelings for me…feelings that I don't reciprocate."

"I kind of got that impression."

"You did? I sure do wish that you would have enlightened me!"

"I guess that I thought that you already knew. I mean, it *was* rather obvious."

"To everyone but me, I guess. No wonder he thinks that I led him on! Did it look to you like I led him on?"

"Not particularly. But you should know that guys interpret things differently than we do. Like, you giving him dancing lessons and asking him to go to the dance."

"What, just because of *that*? I was only trying to help him out of his shell, is all. I could see that he was socially awkward, like I was a few years ago."

"That's how you *meant* it. But Eric *interpreted* it as: 'I think that this girl really likes me.' I guess that even I thought at first that you might have returned his affections, but I wasn't sure. You mean that you were totally oblivious to his feelings?"

"Totally! This is really all new to me. No guys have ever liked me before."

"As far as you know. But I know how you feel. As far as I know, no *girl* has ever liked me before."

Nicole blushed at this remark. She averted her eyes and said:

"So you figured it out. And I tried really hard not to be obvious about it."

"You weren't *too* obvious. Maybe I'm just more perceptive than you are."

"And yet you still want to be friends with me?"

"Of course I do. Don't you still want to be friends with Eric even after discovering his true feelings for you?"

"Yes, but this is different. I know how you born-again-Christian types feel about homosexuality."

"I believe that it's a sin, based what the Bible teaches. But I also believe, again based what the Bible teaches, that we're all sinners. And that certainly includes me! And I also believe that Christians are wrong to treat homosexuality as worse than any other sin and that we are often guilty of treating homosexuals in thoroughly unchristian ways."

"You're a credit to your religion."

"Thank you. Mind you, there is no way I will ever return your affections, either. I *am* a 'born-again-Christian type' as you call it and I'm also totally straight. But we're getting off of the original subject: what happened between Eric and you?"

"He told me how he felt about me and I told him that I didn't feel the same way and then he got angry with me and he started saying all of these horrible things to me, about me."

"I'm afraid that some guys, particularly socially immature ones like Eric, will act that way when they are rebuffed. I've had to deal with this sort of thing myself on some occasions."

"What did you do?" Nicole wondered.

"I prayed for them and then I just got on with my life. You can't be held responsible for someone else' feelings of infatuation, unless you knowingly encouraged it. You have to let the other person deal with their feelings in his or her own way. Sometimes this may mean that you lose a friend over it and sometimes you may gain a closer friendship with the person. You just have to give it some time."

"Thanks for your advice. It's still not going to be easy, though."

"I know. And you've been through so much lately as it is. I'll just have to keep on praying for you."

"Thank you. I'm still not totally convinced about this Christianity thing, but I'm softening on the subject."

"Great! Why don't you come with me to church tonight?"

"You go to church *twice* in one day?"

"And sometimes on Wednesday nights as well."

"Boy, you really are devout!"

"Thank you. But you still haven't answered the question yet."

"Okay, you win. I'll give your church a try."

"Great; the service starts at 7:00 o'clock."

"I can hardly wait." Amy didn't miss the sarcasm in Nicole's voice.

***

The two young ladies arrived at Amy's church at around a quarter to 7:00 p.m. The name of the church was Pleasant Valley Baptist Church. It was a small sized church, certainly not a mega church by any means. Despite its' small size the church hosted a relatively large and thriving 'college and career' group. Amy introduced Nicole to its' members before the service and they all sat together, taking up a couple of rows near the front of the sanctuary.

The church service was all new to Nicole. It started off with music, mostly contemporary Christian choruses with a couple of hymns thrown in for good measure, accompanied by an accomplished ten piece praise band. It wasn't exactly the funeral music that Nicole had expected it to be.

Then they passed around the collection plate. 'Here it comes.' Nicole groaned to herself, 'Pleading for people's money.' But to her surprise, the pastor did not harangue the congregation mercilessly to give until it hurt or else it 'showed a lack of faith.' He simply prayed for the 'offering' and then they passed the plate around. Nicole was impressed; but she still abstained from putting in any money.

Then came the sermon: The young pastor wasn't exactly the fire and brimstone shouter that Nicole had feared that he'd be. In fact, he was not so much a preacher as he was a teacher, expounding the biblical text verse-by-verse, sometimes even word-by-word. He reminded Nicole of some of her better college instructors, though his subject matter wouldn't have been allowed in any modern secular bastion of education!

His text was the Gospel according to John chapter 8, verses 1-11; the story of Jesus and the woman caught in adultery. Nicole had never heard the story before (though she'd often heard the phrase 'he who is without sin, let him cast the first stone' and she always wondered where the saying came from). She couldn't help but think that Jesus sounded a lot more forgiving than many of the Christians that she had known who reminded her more of the Pharisees in the story. Excepting Amy, of course, whom she had the utmost respect for.

After the service the college group went out for dinner at a local restaurant. Nicole was glad that Eric had picked up the tab for lunch because eating out twice a day was definitely an extravagance that her budget couldn't afford (her parents may have been paying for college but they kept her on a tight leash as far as living expenses were concerned). This was not a problem, as it turned out, since the group insisted on paying her way anyway. Nicole protested weakly that she was not a charity case but she was actually happy to accept the offer.

As the group sat around and small talked while looking over their menus Nicole got the distinct impression that the people whom she was supping with knew a great deal more about her than she did about them. Amy had asked Nicole previously if she could have the group pray for her. Nicole was understandably reticent to have her friend divulge any specific information on her trials and tribulations of late to a group of strangers, so Amy just had them pray for her friend at college who was 'having trouble adjusting to college life.'

Nicole was actually touched that these strangers cared enough about her to pray for her, even if she wasn't yet convinced that 'the effectual fervent prayer of a righteous man availeth much' (not that she had ever heard that verse before in her life; not before she met Amy that is). After they had ordered their respective meals, one of the members of the group, a perky blond girl named Liz, inquired:

47

"So, Nicole, what did you think of the sermon?"

"I thought that it was a nice story. I'm not yet ready to accept the veracity of the tale though."

"You know, that section is not in many of the earliest manuscripts."

Observed Brad, who was currently attending Bible College. Amy winced at this remark. She knew that the last thing that you want to discuss around skeptics is disputed Bible passages. She resisted the urge to kick him in the shin from underneath the table and instead propounded:

"I, for one, have no doubt that the section is inspired. What Jesus says to the woman: 'I do not condemn you. Go and sin no more', is the very essence of the gospel message. We are forgiven and now we are empowered by the Holy Spirit to sin no more."

"Do you think that's really possible?" Nicole inquired: "To stop sinning?"

"Theoretically, yes; if we've accepted Jesus Christ as our personal Lord and Savior. Practically...that's another story."

"I'm surprised that someone of your world view even believes in sin."

Brad observed. Nicole answered him:

"Well, I don't know if I agree with everything that the bible calls sin. But I have seen a lot of man's inhumanity towards his fellow man. I would call that a sin."

"Sin is anytime someone acts in their own interest instead of other people's best interest or in God's interest, for that matter." Amy offered.

"That sounds like the way most of us act all of the time." Nicole observed.

"That's why Christ died on the cross for us, Nicole. To change the way that we 'act all of the time' by changing *us*, from the inside out."

There was something so simple and beautiful in what Amy was saying that Nicole felt a tug at her heart to want to believe it. But she just couldn't throw away a lifetime of cynicism at a drop of a hat. Still, it did give her something to think about. Eventually, though, the conversation drifted to less spiritual matters and no one at the table pressed Nicole to make a decision for Christ right there and then.

After supper, the group bid their fond farewells and went their separate ways. As they headed back to the college in Amy's tan 1984 Nissan Sentra, Nicole thanked Amy for having invited her to her church and told her that the experience was better than she had expected. Amy was elated to hear it.

It had been an eventful weekend for Nicole: Besides all of the nocturnal strangeness that she had been experiencing, she had had a bad argument with a new friend and had a bad headache cured by a good friend. She had learned of Eric's true feelings for her and that Amy had divined Nicole's true feelings for her as well. And she was once again confronted with the possibility that God really did exist and that He actually cared for her. All this and two free meals on the same day!

After all that had happened, she was quite ready to go to bed and get some much needed sleep. She was also apprehensive; it was getting to the point where she dreaded going to sleep for fear of what might happen next. But, she also knew that the next day she had classes to go to and some of them were hard enough to stay awake in even with a good night's rest! Not that she even expected to receive a good night's rest anymore. So, she just hopped into bed and hoped for the best.

VIII

Monday November 4th, 1991

Amy woke up around 1 a.m. She tried to get back to sleep but it was no use. After several minutes she gave up and got up. *I might as well check on Nicole* she thought as she put on her robe and slippers. She went down to Nicole's room and quietly opened the door (after all that had been happening lately both girls agreed that it would be prudent for Nicole to leave her door unlocked at night so that Amy could gain easy access).

Amy was not particularly surprised to discover that Nicole was not in her bed; she had come to expect the unexpected where her diminutive friend was concerned. After quickly inspecting the room to ascertain that Nicole was not there, she proceeded down the hall. After a short while, she saw her friend walking slowly down the hallway away from her.

Amy decided to follow Nicole just in case. She watched as Nicole opened the door to the stairwell. Amy could tell after just one quick look at her face that Nicole was sleepwalking. She was also sleeptalking or, rather, sleepmumbling, since Amy couldn't understand a word that she was saying (it sounded like a foreign language, perhaps Latin).

As Nicole walked through the stairway doorway Amy wondered what she should do. She had heard somewhere that it wasn't advisable to wake up someone when they were sleepwalking. On the other hand, she couldn't imagine that walking down a flight of stairs while you were asleep was all that safe, either! She had visions of Nicole sleeptumbling down the stairs. Besides, she didn't fancy following Nicole all over campus; or all over town, if it came to it. So she grabbed Nicole by her slender shoulders and gave her a gentle shake. Nicole awoke disoriented and confused:

"Huh…what…Amy? What are you doing here in my bedroom?"

"Um…I'd hate to break this to you, but…"

"Wait a minute! What are we doing on the landing of the stairs?"

"You were sleepwalking…"

"Oh no! Not again! When will all of this craziness end?"

"Calm down, Nic. Let's be rational about this…"

"How can I possibly be rational about all of this?"

Amy put her arm around Nicole and led her back down the hallway. She noticed that some of the doors of their dorm mates were starting to open up.

"Now we don't want to wake up all of our neighbors again. Now, as I was saying before: we've already determined that your problems are probably either emotional or spiritual."

"That's it; I'm going to see the school counselor today and see if she can recommend a good psychologist…or is it a psychiatrist?"

"You could consider seeing my pastor. He'd probably do it for free."

"Maybe. I'll try anything to end all this!" The two girls went into Nicole's room, shut the door and sat down upon the bed. Amy cautioned:

"It may take awhile to get down to the bottom of your problem."

"I don't care! I can't take this anymore! I'm afraid to even go to sleep anymore!"

"You've just got to hang on. There's got to be a reason why all this is happening to you. We've just got to be patient."

"It's easy for you to say that! It's not happening to *you*!"

Immediately after her angry outburst, Nicole was racked by feelings of guilt.

"Oh, Amy…I'm so sorry. And after you've been so sweet to me…"

"Forget it. You're just stressed out. I would be too if it was happening to me."

"You're so understanding."

"I'm also so tired. We'd better both get some sleep before classes."

"Thanks for keeping an eye on me. I might have been halfway to downtown if you hadn't caught me."

***

About four hours later Nicole was rudely awakened by her alarm clock and, after hitting the snooze several times, she drug her tired little body out of bed. She was too late for a shower so she quickly got dressed, combed her hair and ran off to grab some breakfast before her first class. She went through classes like a zombie, the last few nights taking their toll on her physically as well as emotionally.

She saw Eric from time to time around campus but she didn't know what to do. She longed to patch things up with him but she was afraid of how he would react. So she would just quickly look away and quickened her pace onto her next destination. Between classes she talked to the school counselor about her problems of late and got some advice (like getting some sleeping pills), as well as some names of practitioners of the mental health profession.

After classes and eating supper in the cafeteria, she went to the library and attempted to work on a Sociology term paper that was soon to be due that she hadn't even started on yet! She was not a procrastinator by nature but with all that had been happening to her for the last few days (or, to be more accurate, the last few nights) she hadn't been able to focus on any of her subjects; not even the ones that she enjoyed like Sociology.

But it was no use; she was just too tired. Her head ached dully and she couldn't get her mind to focus on anything. So she grabbed her books, drowsily walked back to her dorm, went upstairs to her room and collapsed upon the bed. It was not her habit to go to bed that early and she knew that she was only asking for trouble considering her recent experiences in bed but she was just too tired to care! She soon fell asleep.

***

Nicole woke up suddenly and looked around her dorm room. The first thing that she saw was her stuffed toy devil. Except that it didn't look like her stuffed toy devil anymore, it looked more menacing, more evil. She got out of bed and picked up the devil, looking at it closely; she had a crazy idea that it held the secret to everything that had been happening to her. Suddenly, she was no longer in her dorm room but in Mr. Spencer's store, still dressed in her nightgown and still clutching the stuffed devil.

Then she noticed that the devil was getting heavier. When she looked down at it she saw that it was growing. Nicole also observed that it was no longer a stuffed toy at all but instead she saw that the plush fabric had changed to scaly skin; it had become a real devil! Then she noticed that its' face had also changed: it now had Eric's face! Nicole tried to scream but she could not even speak; she tried to run away but she couldn't even move!

The Eric/devil just laughed, then it reached out one of its' scaly red hands and grasped Nicole by her shoulder. Nicole tried to pry the hand off of her but it was too strong! After a few moments of struggling she noticed that demon's hand had metamorphosized into a delicate human hand and the face had also altered into the pretty face of Amy Daniels, who was saying:

"Wake up, Nicole, you were having another nightmare."

"Dreaming and screaming, I'll bet. Did I wake everybody up again?"

"No, I woke you up in time. Besides, it's still early in the evening and you know that college students never go to bed *this* early! Do you remember your dream this time? It may help us to get down to the bottom of the problem."

"I-I'll try…sorry, there's nothing…wait a minute, I'm starting to remember something…vaguely. Something to do with my stuffed devil…its' face…now I remember: it had Eric's face!"

"Eric's face?"

"Yes! What does it mean?"

"You're getting excited again, calm down."

"Calm down? How can I? I just don't understand why all of this is happing to me! Either I'm cracking up or I'm starring in Exorcist IV! I just can't take this anymore!"

All at once Nicole broke down; she buried her head in Amy's bosom and cried like a baby: releasing all of her pent up anger and fear. Amy put her arms around her and lovingly stroked her hair, telling her 'It's all right, let it all out.' Nicole didn't like giving herself away liked this; she liked to maintain some semblance of control. But she just couldn't help herself; it just felt so good to let herself go. After a good cry, Nicole attempted to compose herself.

"I...I'm sorry, Amy. You must think that I'm some kind of hysterical nut."

"Not at all, this must be a very trying experience for you. But I think that there's something that we should consider."

"What's that?"

"Perhaps your dream was significant."

"In what way?" Nicole wondered aloud.

"Nicole...how well do you know Eric?" Amy asked.

"What are you implying?"

"What I'm implying is: Eric is a mysterious and odd fellow: Maybe he really *is* behind all of this."

"But how?"

"Maybe he's into the occult."

"You're crazy! Besides, I don't believe in all of that."

"I know that you don't; but *I* do. Just hear me out on this matter. It would explain an awful lot of what's been happening to you. And I still think that it's all tied up in that stuffed devil that you were sent."

"But Eric's an atheist." Nicole asserted.

"Or so he *says*." Amy countered.

"But why would Eric do all of this to me?"

"Maybe to make you dependent upon him."

"But...if he was doing all of this because he thought that he loved me, what's he going to do to me now that I've rejected him?"

"Now *that* is a truly scary thought."

Just then there was a knock at Nicole's door. She opened it to see the unsmiling face of one of her dorm sisters, Karen McGill. Ever since Nicole's nighttime ailments began there had been a slow eroding of harmonious relations between Nicole and her dorm mates. Even the most understanding of her co-eds were growing tired of her 'histrionics' and some of the less understanding of them (like Miss McGill) were going so far as to imply that Nicole was doing all of it just to gain attention. By now, Amy was the only one on the entire hall who was still on speaking terms with Nicole.

"Phone." Karen said curtly.

'What now.' Nicole thought as she made her way to the community telephone on her hall. As Nicole was picking up the receiver Karen couldn't resist lobbing a parting shot at Nicole before she slipped into her dorm room:

"Don't start screaming into the phone or pull the phone off of the wall while you're sleepwalking."

Nicole just ignored Karen's jibes and spoke into the receiver:

"H-hello?"

"Nicole?"

"Mom!"

"Good evening, Nicole. How is college life agreeing with you?"

"Disagreeing with me is more like it."

"I can tell; you sound tired. Are you getting enough sleep?"

"No; and while were on that subject: I'm glad you called because I wanted to ask you something."

"What do you want to know?" Nicole's mother asked apprehensively.

"Have you ever known me to talk in my sleep or…to sleepwalk?"

"No, I haven't. But something in your voice tells me that you have a good reason to ask those questions."

"I do; according to my dorm mates I have been doing a lot of strange things in my sleep lately. And there's more: I've been having the most horrible nightmares!"

"You're worrying me. What are your dreams about?"

"I don't really remember; something about the devil or hell or something like that. But they must be really bad because…I've been told that I have woken up screaming!"

"Now I'm *really* concerned about you."

"So am I. Mom…have I ever had any traumatic experiences growing up that I may have blocked out?"

"Heaven's no!" Anne Marie exclaimed.

"I also have to ask you this: is there any history of mental illness in our family?"

"Certainly not! You're just worried about college, is all."

"That's what I thought at first but it's happening *every* night! Amy seems to think that it's supernatural in nature."

"Amy is that fanatic that your friends with, isn't she? Of course she's going to say that. That's the way those people always think."

"Amy is *not* a fanatic! She's a very level-headed girl. And the people at her church seemed perfectly normal."

"Her church? Don't tell me that you're being indoctrinated into her Christian beliefs. No wonder you're having nightmares!"

"For your information: the nightmares started *before* I visited her church."

"Then it's due to all of her preaching at you about hell. That's what those people do! You yourself said that you're dreaming about hell and the devil and all of those types of things that we don't believe in."

"I wish that you'd stop using the term 'those people'. I thought that you didn't believe in stereotyping; or doesn't that apply to Christians?"

"You're right." Nicole's mother admitted after a pause. "I'm being intolerant and you called me on it."

"Nobody's perfect, Mom. Look, I don't want to argue with you. I just wanted to get some answers."

"I don't want to argue either. But I *am* worried about you. But, no, I have no explanation whatsoever as to why all of this is happening to you. Have you spoken with a psychiatrist yet?"

"I spoke with the school counselor. She recommended some people to me."

"That's good. But, I'm sure that the college doesn't want me to tie up the phone line any longer. Goodbye, darling. I love you and I hope that you get over whatever it is that's bothering you as soon as possible."

"So do I. Love you to, mom. Goodbye."

Nicole would have asked her mother to pray for her if her mother believed in such things. She went back to her room where Amy was still waiting for her.

"It was just my mom." Nicole explained. "According to her all of my nocturnal behaviors as of late are latent manifestations."

"This just strengthens my argument that your problem is supernatural in nature."

"I'm beginning to believe that you may be right. But right now I'm going to go back to bed, which proves that I must be a masochist."

"Good night." Amy wished.

"I sure hope so." Nicole replied wearily as she got back into bed.

IX

Tuesday November 5th, 1991

Nicole woke up the next morning feeling at least a little better than yesterday morn. She even managed to stay awake during even her most boring of classes (and some of them were excruciatingly boring!). She once again avoided Eric like the plague. After her conversation with Amy last night, she was more reluctant than ever to speak to him. Eric, however, had other ideas and accosted her in the hall way between classes. As Nicole steeled herself for the worst, Eric spoke:

"I need to talk to you."

"A-all right, Eric." She said apprehensively.

"I wanted to apologize for what I said to you on Sunday. I realize that I was being unfair."

"I accept your apology. But you must also accept that I was very hurt by the things that you said."

"I'm sorry; but you hurt me, too, inadvertently though it may have been."

"I can't be held responsible for your feelings. I didn't mean to lead you on."

"I know that you didn't. If only you didn't look so pretty…"

"Thank you. But I can't help *that* either."

"I'm sorry that I was unfair."

"It *is* unfair for guys to say that a girl is a...witch, for want of a better word, if she doesn't want to go out with them."

"I never said that; but I am sorry for what I *did* say."

"Let's just pretend it never happened then."

"The old 'let's just be friends' routine, huh?"

"If you're willing to settle for that."

"I'd still rather have you for a girlfriend than a friend but I'll settle for what I can get."

"Friends then." Nicole said as she hugged Eric, "and, of course, Biology I study buddies."

"I knew that you were only using me for my brains."

***

Nicole went back to her dorm room feeling better about Eric. They had had a good conversation and had succeeded in clearing the air between them. Still, she didn't altogether trust him. Amy had certainly planted some seeds of doubt in her mind. Nicole sat on her bed and looked up at the stuffed devil. It suddenly occurred to her that she had never asked Eric if he had sent it back when she had first received it because they hadn't known each other back then. Obviously, if Eric *was* behind it all he would only deny it. Still, she decided to call him and ask him to meet her and find out once and for all.

At any rate, she decided to get rid of the devil anyway. Whether or not Amy was correct in her assumptions, Nicole was starting to become creeped out by the thing. She called Eric's dorm but he wasn't in. She went to dinner, hoping to find Eric there, but no such luck. After eating at the cafeteria she went back to her dorm room, then she called Eric's hall again and, once she got him on the phone, asked him to meet with her as soon as possible. She then threw the stuffed toy in her backpack and then met Eric outside the women's dormitory that very evening.

"Hi, Nicole. What did you want to discuss with me?"

Nicole pulled out the stuffed devil and asked him:

"What do you make of this?"

"Looks like a stuffed toy. If that's a gift for me, it's a strange one."

"No, actually, it was a gift for *me*, an anonymous one. I received it around Halloween."

"Looks like something that my father would have in his shop."

"Quite. Eric, I want to ask you a question and I want you to be perfectly honest with me."

"Certainly. What's the question?"

"Did you send it? It's okay if you did. It's only that a lot of strange things have been happening to me ever since I received it."

"No, Nicole, I did *not* send it. What do you mean by strange things?"

"Nightmares, sleep walking, headaches."

Nicole quickly explained some of the things that she had been going through. Eric seemed both concerned and alarmed. If he *was* behind it all he was sure putting on a good act. Suddenly, Nicole started getting another headache; if possible, this one was even worse than the one before! She dropped the toy and her backpack and grabbed her head.

"Ow! Oh, no, not again!"

"What's wrong?"

"Headache...worst than the last one! Amy helped last time...but tonight...she's out on a date. She seems to think...that...it's a...supernatural problem."

"I agree. And if that is true, it follows that the solution must be supernatural as well."

"I thought you...were an atheist."

"I said that I was an atheist when I was younger but not for the last few years, not after some of the things that I've seen in my life. Or, at least, I believe in the supernatural, if not actually in a benevolent heavenly Father. And I know someone who may be able to help you."

With that he grabbed Nicole by the hand and grabbed the devil with his other one. She still didn't wholly trust Eric but she was now in too much pain to care. She also figured that if he was the cause of all of her troubles, then he could also be the cure. It occurred to her that this could have been his design all along: to make her dependent on him and/or so that he could save her from all of her miseries and thus appear to be her 'knight in shining armor'.

At this point Nicole was so tired of the fight, and so tired of the pain, that she would have gone to hell with the devil himself if it would end her suffering once and for all. She got into Eric's car and he drove downtown to his father's store. Considering her last dream, this did *not* exactly inspire her confidence! The store was closed but Mr. Spencer opened the door, greeting Nicole in his usual jovial manner.

"Miss Nicholson, so good to see you again. My, but you don't look well at all. Have a headache?"

"No thanks…already have one."

Eric quickly brought his father up to speed on the situation.

"Sounds like someone put a spell on you." The elder Spencer pondered.

"What is this…the dark ages?" Nicole groaned.

"Can you help her, father?" Eric asked hopefully.

"Certainly, I can. Firstly, I'll cure that nasty headache."

Mr. Spencer laid his hands on Nicole's throbbing forehead and started speaking in a low voice. At first Nicole figured that he was praying, as Amy had done. But these words she couldn't begin to understand. It sounded like Latin to her. Whatever his incantation, it soon had the desired effect. Nicole's headache soon subsided. Just like the last time she also felt something of a presence, though this time it was more of a malevolent one.

Nicole exclaimed:

"Amazing! I don't know how you mystic types do it."

"Meaning that your headache is gone?" Eric asked Nicole.

"Yes, Eric. Thank you, Mr. Spencer."

"You are most welcome. But, pardon me, what did you mean by 'mystic types': plural?"

"Oh, I was just talking about a friend of mine who cured my last splitting headache. Are you a Christian too?"

"Hardly." Edmund laughed.

"But, father, you've only fixed the immediate problem. What about the rest of the symptoms?" Eric reminded his father.

"I believe that I can aid you in that as well. There are certain incantations that I know of; certain counteracting spells."

"But, father, didn't you once tell me that some spells can only be broken by the person who first cast it."

"That is true." Mr. Spencer answered.

"But we don't know who cast it."

"I don't care!" Nicole exclaimed. "I just want it to end!"

"Patience, my child. Now, Miss Nicholson, do you have any enemies, perhaps?" Mr. Spencer inquired.

"I had several in grade school up through high school. But none who hated me enough to put me through this living hell!"

"Maybe the person has another motive?" Eric observed.

"How very astute, my son. Do you have any suggestions…love perhaps?"

At this, Nicole glanced up at Eric. Eric winced and said:

"No one who truly loved someone would do this to them. Nicole's right, though: this surmising is pointless. We still don't know who is doing this or why."

"Oh, contraire, my dear son. I know the answer to both of those questions. Now, whoever cast the spell must have had knowledge of the black arts." Edmund proposed with an evil smile.

At this suggestion, Eric looked aghast at his father. His father just laughed. Eric exclaimed:

"Father, how could you?"

"But why, Mr. Spencer?" Nicole asked "I've never even met you until last week."

"You see, Miss Nicholson, when I converted to Satanism my son and I had a falling out. Religious differences, you see. You might say that he became a prodigal son. I wanted him back. I found an opportunity this autumn when I learned that the poor fool had lost his heart to a fair young maiden. Namely: you."

"I really *was* the last one to know." Nicole observed painfully.

"Quite. I actually knew as early as September. Eric was talking *about* you long before he developed enough courage to speak *to* you. Now, as soon as I knew about my son's silly infatuation for you I thought of a way that I could use it to my advantage. I figured that I could get to my son through you."

"I…I thought that you were my friend. You were just using me!"

"How very naïve of you, Miss Nicholson."

"I'm ashamed to call you my father." Eric said ashamedly.

"And I'm ashamed to call a sniveling weakling like you my son. I don't need your petty moralizing. I have *power*!"

"All right, father, so you have us over a barrel. Now, how about helping Nicole?"

"Certainly. Only one small request: you must promise to follow in my footsteps."

"Don't do it Eric! Don't let him corrupt you like he is!" Nicole warned.

"The alternative is not very pleasant, at least not for *you*, wench! I rather enjoy practicing sympathetic magick. And I promise you, Eric, that I could make your little friend's life a veritable hell on earth that would make the last few days seem like paradise in comparison."

"How can anyone be so evil?" Nicole gasped.

"It's easy when you dispense with the concept of good and evil. So, Eric: I am still awaiting your answer."

"All right, curse you, I agree."

"Eric, no! Don't let him win!" Nicole pleaded.

"I have to; I can't allow you to go through anymore pain."

"I counted on that, my tenderhearted son. Now follow me."

Mr. Spencer produced the skeleton key from his sweater pocket and opened the same door in the back of the store that he had for Nicole the other day. Mr. Spencer then motioned for the two of them to follow him. He walked past the office area and then opened up another door, behind which were creaking, rickety stairs that led down to an ancient looking cellar.

To Nicole's surprise it was not cobweb infested and neglected, it was obviously still used on a regular basis. At the foot of the stairs there was an antique bookcase with a myriad of books on witchcraft and the occult, as well as candles and potions and even a (living) black cat. Also on the shelf was a stuffed toy devil that looked exactly like Nicole's. She gasped. Mr. Spencer laughed and explained:

"Oh yes, Miss Nicholson, it was *I* who sent you the toy devil. In fact, it was I who made it. But it isn't a toy; it is a vessel of my power. I used it to make you suffer."

"So that's why everything that was happening to me happened while I was near the devil. And that explains why the last headache was the worse because I was holding the devil!"

"Precisely."

"But if your power is tied to the object, what's to stop me from just destroying it?"

"You weren't listening. Only the person who cast the spell can break it. And I will never break it."

"But you promised, father." Eric reminded.

"I lied. Oh, I won't torment the poor girl anymore, as long as you obey me in all things. But if you rebel against me again I shall bring all the powers of hell to bear upon her! In other words, Miss Nicholson shall be my insurance policy to keep you in line. You may go your way now, wench, my son and I have much to discuss. (Nicole hesitated) I said go!"

"Here, Nicole, take my car." Eric said as he handed her the keys.

***

Nicole reluctantly drove Eric's car back to the college; she would rather have been in constant excruciating pain than to have Eric subject to his father's monstrous will. But she noticed that the devil was still in Eric's car. Is that why he suggested that she take his car? Did he think that she could somehow destroy it? Or was it just a coincidence?

Nicole went back up to her dorm room and just sat on her bed feeling numb. She tried to pray to the God that she claimed that she didn't even believe in but she didn't know if it did any good owing to her lack of faith. Then she heard a knock on her door, she opened it to Amy's smiling face. Her prayer had been answered!

Amy confided to her as soon as she entered:

"I just had the most wonderful date with…wait, what's wrong Nicole?"

Nicole hurriedly related what had transpired that evening.

"I *knew* that I shouldn't have taken the night off and gone out on a date!"

"Forget about that Amy, what are we going to do?"

"We need to end the curse but still extricate Eric from his father's clutches."

"But how?" Nicole asked.

"Spencer was either lying or misinformed when he said that the spell could only be revoked by the one who cast it."

"What do you mean?"

"I mean, unlike in life, good always triumphs over evil in the supernatural realm."

"Who are you, Pollyanna?"

"Just listen: with God on our side we should be able to revoke the spell. The trouble began when you received that package. From what you have told me, I was right when I surmised that it was all linked to the stuffed devil."

"You mean that all we have to do is destroy the toy?"

"Yes, but it's not quite that simple. I believe that the power of this spell is centered in the toy devil, but it ultimately comes from the *real* devil. Jesus Christ came to defeat the power of the devil. Demons tremble at the very mention of His name. I believe that destroying the devil may break Mr. Spencer's spell on you but you are still under the power of Satan. The Bible states that all people are under his power until we are spiritually regenerated by the Holy Spirit. It's time that you made a decision about what you believe."

Nicole thought about what she *did* in fact believe. She could no longer deny that the supernatural world existed. It made sense that if there was an ultimate force for evil then there had to be an ultimate force for good as well. She had seen the effects of following the power of evil like Mr. Spencer had; she had also seen the power for good in people like Amy. There was no doubt in her mind which side she wanted to be on, even if it wasn't (contrary to what Amy claimed) the winning side.

"What do I have to do?" She asked.

"The Bible says that we are all born spiritually dead and we are all born sinners. Christ died on the cross to pay for our sins. You just have to admit that you are a sinner and accept Jesus Christ as your personal Lord and Savior."

Nicole thought about it. She had always thought that she had been more sinned against than sinning. But she also realized that she was no angel herself. She had hated her classmates for years for what they had done to her. She closed her eyes and prayed as Amy had instructed her, feeling like a parrot repeating the words. Did she really believe it? Yes, she realized, in fact, she did. As she was praying she felt similar to how she felt when Amy had prayed over her. After she was done praying she felt different.

Then she opened her eyes and looked at Amy who inquired:

"How do you feel?"

"Different, like I finally know what 'joy' is. Okay, now what?"

"Do you still have that devil?"

"It's in Eric's car in the parking lot."

***

The two of them got into Eric's car and headed to a nearby convenience store, where they procured a lighter, lighter fluid and a small metal wastebasket. They took these items back to the dorm and placed the devil in the wastebasket, doused it in fluid and then Amy handed the lighter to Nicole, telling her:

"You do the honors."

"Gladly."

Nicole lit the object, and as the toy devil went up in flames, Amy prayed:

"Heavenly Father, Your word tells us that greater is He that is in us than he that is in the world and that Christ came to destroy the works of the devil. I pray that Your power will break this satanic spell and release Your child Nicole from its' evil grip. In Jesus' name I pray. Amen."

The toy devil was soon consumed. The question remained: had it really worked? There was only one way to find out: the two of them jumped into Eric's car and drove down to Spencer's store. Eric met them at the door and then inquired as he let them in:

"Nicole, what are you and Amy doing here?"

"We're here to rescue you." Nicole explained.

"You know that that's impossible."

Suddenly, Edmund Spencer appeared behind Eric.

"So, it appears that I was not clear enough in my demonstration of my power. No matter, I will simply have to impress upon you the consequences of disobedience. Even without the benefit of the stuffed devil I still have enough power, being in such close proximity to you, to work my will."

Spencer then stared intently and gestured menacingly at Nicole and conjured: "And so, now: intense pain!"

Nicole braced herself for another one of those excruciating headaches or an even worse onslaught. To her surprise, she felt nothing. In relief her face broke out in a smile. Edmund Spencer exclaimed in disbelief:

"Inconceivable! By now you should be writhing in agony!"

"She is now a child of God," Amy explained "You no longer have any power over her!"

"I curse your impotent god!" Edmund exclaimed, "My Satan is far stronger!"

"You're wrong, and I'll prove it." Amy looked intensely into Mr. Spencer's eyes and confidently pronounced: "In the name of the Lord Jesus Christ, I command the unclean spirit to come out of you!"

Suddenly, Mr. Spencer's body convulsed and he let out a scream. The three other people in the room could feel something like an evil presence come out of the man and exit the building. Gone was the confident, urbane Edmund Spencer; what remained was a tired looking, worn out old man. After a stunned silence, Eric turned to Amy and asked her:

"How did you do that?"

"It's easy when you're aligned with the *real* power in the universe!"

"Now, Father, will you please renounce Satan?" Eric pleaded.

"And accept Jesus Christ?" Amy added.

"Never!" Edmund shouted defiantly.

"What should we do with him?" Nicole wondered.

"I doubt that the police will believe any of this." Eric offered.

"At least he is powerless now." Amy prognosticated.

"Good!" Nicole cheered, "At last I'm free of him!"

"So am I." Eric echoed.

"Don't bet on it, son!" Mr. Spencer warned as he ran back to his office. "I'll fix all of you someday."

"Let him go, Eric" Amy counseled. "He no longer has any spiritual hold on Nicole. You, on the other hand…"

"It appears that I will have to change my theological views."

"Let's discuss this somewhere else." Nicole suggested as she handed Eric back his car keys. "Now this place just gives me the creeps!"

As they drove back to campus, Amy began to disclose to Eric the way of salvation through Jesus Christ's death on the cross. Having seen enough evidence of the supernatural and the triumph of good over evil, Eric readily accepted Jesus Christ as his Lord and Savior by the time they got back to college.

X

Wednesday November 6ᵗʰ, 1991

Nicole awoke the next morning having enjoyed the best night of sleep she had had in nearly a week. No more nightmares, headaches, etc; she had not even so much as awoke in the middle of the night to use the restroom. She also felt like she was a new creation; which, in fact, she was.

The only problem was that her dreaded Biology I class had a post mid term/pre-final exam test today and with everything that had happened to her yesterday she had neither the time nor the inclination to study for it. Luckily, last night, before they had parted, Eric and she agreed to meet in the usual place, the student lounge, for an emergency cram session.

So, Nicole got up earlier than usual, got dressed and performed the most perfunctory of grooming functions and then raced to the student lounge. After the cram session she went off to the exam. If only Biology I wasn't her first class that day, she would have had more time to prepare!

But Nicole said a quick prayer (something she was *not* in the habit of doing) before she started the test and she was flooded with a sense of peace. Then she took the exam, did her best and hoped for the best. She worked all the way up to the bell and then reluctantly handed in her test. After class she saw Eric waiting for her outside the classroom.

"So, Eric, you finished up pretty quickly."

"I see that you didn't. How do you think you did?"

"Better than I would have thought; thanks to your tutelage. I feel pretty good about it. In fact, I feel pretty good period: physically, mentally and spiritually speaking."

"I'm glad to hear it. You've had enough stress in your life lately."

"What a week I've been having! But it was all worth it to gain the peace that I now have with God."

"I agree. It's wonderful isn't it?"

"Yes, Eric, it is. I never imagined that when I saw you staring at me in the student lounge that day that you would become not only a good friend but a Christian brother as well."

"I have a confession to make: I had actually been staring at you for a couple of months by that time, ever since I first saw you on that first day in Biology I class. It just took you that long to notice."

"Love at first sight, huh? Well, I'll be; as far as I know no one's ever worshipped me from afar before."

"As far as you know, but I wouldn't be surprised if you hadn't had a plethora of secret admirers in your lifetime. But now we both *worship* the *right* Object."

***

Nicole gave Eric a fraternal hug and went off to her other classes, after which she practically skipped back to her dormitory. She decided that she'd better call home since her parents were no doubt worried sick about her. She decided to use the pay phone this time. When she called home her father answered the phone.

"Hello? Nicholson's residence."

"Daddy!"

"Nicole! How is my favorite girl?"

"I'm your *only* girl and to answer your question: I feel much better."

"That's good to hear. You know, your mother and I were getting quite concerned about these sleeping disorders of yours."

"So was I but I think that the problem has been solved."

"So soon? How?"

"You wouldn't believe me if I told you."

"Try me."

"Okay, but in order for you to believe it you would have to believe in the supernatural."

"Which I don't. Your mother also made mention about this new found interest that you've developed in…Christianity of all things!"

"It's worse than you think: last night I accepted Jesus Christ as my personal Lord and Savior!"

"Oh, dear Lord!" Nicolas exclaimed.

"Yes, dad, He has become *very* dear to me. You probably haven't been this disappointed in me as when you found out that I was going to be born a girl."

"Now, Nicole, your mother and I have always loved you. I couldn't be any more proud of you than if you'd been my son."

"Thanks, daddy. It means so much to me to hear you say that."

"I mean it. But this Christianity thing…"

"Oh, come on, dad; most parents are afraid of their children *losing* their faith when they go off to college!"

"Still, if you were going to 'get religion' couldn't it at least be Buddhism or Hinduism; Christianity is so politically incorrect. And it's so much against everything that your mother and I believe in."

"Sorry, dad; blame it on the Holy Spirit."

"So what does this all have to do with curing your sleep disorders?"

"It turns out that the causes *were* supernatural in nature…"

"I think that you were just worried about your classes."

"Speaking of which: I think I might have even passed my Biology I test today!"

"That's great! That's the class that you were struggling in, wasn't it?"

"Yep. But in another month and a half it will all be over. Then I just need to worry about Zoology…and Algebra…and…"

"Don't worry, you'll get through it. I have faith in you."

"More importantly: I now have faith in God."

"Your mother is not going to believe this 'conversion' of yours."

"Speaking of mother: why don't you put her on the phone?"

"Because she's out Christmas shopping already."

"That's my mom: she doesn't even wait until the day after Thanksgiving! She sure makes a lot of fuss over the birth of a Person that she doesn't even believe in."

"We believe that Jesus was good moral teacher, that is all. But speaking of Thanksgiving: you are coming home for that weekend, I assume?"

"You should never assume. But, in this case, you assume correctly: I wouldn't miss it for the world. Just don't forget the stuffing!"

"We won't. But this call is costing you money."

"Hint taken. Then goodbye for now. I love you and give mom my love."

"Love you too, honey."

***

After phoning home Nicole went to her room and flopped down upon the bed; finally able to relax on the very piece of furniture that she had been getting to the point of dreading even using at all. Shortly thereafter she heard Amy's familiar knock at her door. When Nicole had granted permission for her to enter, Amy came in, sat down on the bed beside Nicole and inquired:

"So, how did you sleep last night?"

"Better than I have in almost a week!" Nicole answered as she sat up.

"That's great!"

"Yes, it is. Speaking of which: thank you once again for looking out for me last week."

"What are friends for? Besides, I think that it was really the Lord that was looking out for you. I mean, I've never woken up in the middle of the night so much before in my entire life! I don't think that it's a coincidence."

"You mean Divine Intervention?"

"It's definitely possible. However, I hate to say this, considering all that you've been through, both in the past week and while growing up; but I would caution you not to think that now that you're a Christian that everything's going to be a walk in the park. In fact, in some ways, your life is going to get a lot harder; now Satan is really going to be gunning for you."

"I realize that; after all, I'm still going to be living in this world of trials and tribulations."

"Speaking of trials and tribulations: how did the Biology I test go today?"

"I think I may even have passed it."

"That's good news."

"The *real* good news is that now I'm 'saved'!"

"I agree." Amy said giving Nicole a hug. "Now we're not only best friends; we are sisters in the Lord!"

"I guess that's as close as we'll ever be, so I'll take it."

"You can take this as well." Amy handed her a wrapped present.

Nicole tore the wrapping paper off and found a New King James version of the Holy Bible. She exclaimed:

"Oh, Amy, you shouldn't have!"

"Why not? You're my best friend. Besides you're going to need to bone up on your biblical knowledge if you're going to have a victorious Christian life. Just think of it as your first 'spiritual' birthday gift."

"Okay. After all, it's a lot better than that anonymous gift that I had received last month!"